The pleasure of your company is requested at

The Butterfly Ball

and

The Grasshopper's Feast

to be held beneath the Broad Oak Tree

RSVP
The Organisers,
The Butterfly Ball,
Broad Oak Tree.

Fancy Dress optional.
(Wasps, Hornets and Bees
are requested to leave
their stings at home.)

THIS IS THE TALE of the summer's day, deep in the woods of England, when the Butterflies and Grasshoppers invited all the creatures of air and land to a Ball and Feast. From St Michael's Mount, Windsor, Rye, Salisbury, Tintern Abbey and the far corners of Britain they came – moles, gnats, dormice, newts, shrews, caterpillars, moths, frogs, squirrels, spiders, toads, mice, bees, flies, worms, centipedes, hares, hedgehogs, otters and foxes. Setting out in Johnson's Spinner Trains, hot-air balloons, stagecoaches and on foot, most arrive – some fall foul of bats, stoats, wasps and foxes and don't! Beneath the Broad Oak Tree the Butterflies and guests dance the evening away, feasting and merrymaking until the glow-worms light up and lead the weary guests back to their beds.

THE
BUTTERFLY BALL

— AND —

THE GRASSHOPPER'S FEAST

Alan Aldridge

WITH VERSES BY
William Plomer

AND NATURE NOTES BY
Richard Fitter

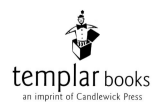

templar books
an imprint of Candlewick Press

Text and illustrations copyright © 1973 by Alan Aldridge
Verses copyright © 1973 by The Estate of William Plomer
Nature Notes by Richard Fitter
"Alan Aldridge and *The Butterfly Ball*" by Oliver Craske
Design by Palazzo Editions Ltd.

First Candlewick Press edition 2009

Library of Congress Cataloging-in-Publication Data is available.
Library of Congress Catalog Card Number 2008935209
ISBN 978-0-7636-4422-2

2 4 6 8 10 9 7 5 3 1

Printed in China

This book was typeset in Monkton.
The twenty-eight color plates by Alan Aldridge were prepared
in collaboration with Harry Willock.

Nature Notes engravings:
Alamy/Alan King (76 top); Fotosearch (70, 81, 88 bottom);
Mary Evans Picture Library (68, 80, 87 bottom, 88 top, and 89).

A TEMPLAR BOOK
an imprint of
Candlewick Press
99 Dover Street
Somerville, Massachusetts 02144
www.candlewick.com

CONTENTS

This is the Day!

AS NIGHT turns to dimness and draws back its curtain,
Stars, those bright sequins, now all disappear,
As dimness grows radiant, dawn makes it certain
That butterfly weather, quite perfect, is here;

Thundery cumulus masses are drifting
Very far off; overhead, very high,
Cirrus clouds spread their pink feathers, then lifting,
Dissolve and are lost in the turquoise-blue sky;

Up comes the Sun, and the very long shadows
Grow shorter; his light is like amber; the glow,
Where grey mists have melted away from the meadows,
Starts dewdrops all sparkling like jewels below;

Creatures that fly, or that creep, hop, or run,
Now wake all at once at a loud trumpet-call
To tell them this greatest of days has begun –
The day of the Feast and the Butterfly Ball!

At the sound of the trumpet the dozens invited
Now jump out of bed, squealing, "This is the day!
Oh, goody! The Ball! Aren't you madly excited?
Get up and get ready! Let's be on our way!"

Harold the Herald

ANTARA, teroo!
  I'm Harold the Herald,
    Gadfly and trumpeter too,
  Well equipped for my job, as you see.
  My trumpet's a gentian,
  My sword's in its scabbard,
  My wife, let me mention,
  Embroidered my tabard
With stitches as fine as can be.

  Tantara, teroo!
  Wake up and take notice,
  This news is important for you!
  Today is a great day for all
  In the insect creation
  (And that is a rhyme for Jollification),
  So do be in time for
The magnificent Butterfly Ball!

PS   *At dawn, when sunshine with a flood*
     Of light fills all the sky with gold,
     The Gadfly's wife (so I've been told)
     Besides the paper and the post
     Brings him a morning cup of blood,
     Not just because he likes it most;
     It is in fact his only food
     And puts him in a sanguine mood
     For doing almost anything,
     But most of all for trumpeting.

PLATE 1

Mrs Dormouse

A DORMOUSE is a sleepy mouse
But this is not a sleepy house,
It's Honeysuckle Hall,
And Saffron Dormouse and her son
(His name is Tom) are full of fun,
They're going to the Ball.

Yesterday she washed her hair
(All over) knowing she would wear
Today her smartest thing,
Her picture hat heaped up with fruit;
Tom has put on his sailor suit
And she her ruby ring.

Dormice in winter like to snooze,
Not now! Look at her party shoes,
And oh, what lovely eyes!
Her husband married her because
He thought her finest feature was
Their lustre and their size.

PLATE 2

Old Blind Mole

AMONG his home-made tunnels is the deep, dark hole,
The secret home and hide-out of Old Blind Mole,
And as he's not a tidy Mole
It's not a tidy hidey-hole.
It's dusty, musty, dingy, and on the floor he scatters
Half-chewed scraps of worms and things; he doesn't think it matters.

Now to him, deep underground,
Faintly there comes a thrilling sound –
Harold the Herald's trumpet call
Announcing that tonight's the Ball!

Up gets Mole to brush his sleeves
Free from earth and bits of leaves;
Meaning today to look his best
Before he went to bed he pressed
Under his mattress with much care
The velvet coat he means to wear.

He slips it on, puts on his hat,
Takes up his stick; as for his lunch,
He has no worry about that –
A bunch of juicy worms to munch.

PLATE 3

Dandy Rat and the Footpads

ALONG the seashore near St Michael's Mount,
The sea quite calm beneath a mild blue sky,
On his high-stepping grey so proud and smart
Rich Dandy Rat, the merchant, canters by.

With satin saddle-cloth and silver spurs,
Silk, lace and feathers, feeling at his best,
Much looking forward to the Ball tonight,
To being admired because superbly dressed,

"How fine I am!" he thinks, "I only wish
The crew could see me from that ship becalmed."
All in a flash he finds himself attacked
By four fierce footpads, dangerously armed.

With pitchfork, cutlass, and goat-headed club
There's Oswald Otter, What's-his-name the Stoat,
Reynard DeAth the Fox, and Barney Bat –
They mean to rob him and then cut his throat.

They drag him down, they grab his cloak and sword,
Tear off his clothes, and find his heavy purse.
Out roll gold coins! While over these they fight
Dandy, like lightning, fearing something worse,

Darts through the bushes, racing for his life,
Not mounted now, nor dressed up for the Ball.
When he arrives there, somebody will squeak
"Disgraceful! Dandy Rat's got nothing on at all!"

PS. *Before you turn over, here's a good game –*
Hunt through the picture and find out Stoat's name.

(The answer is on the last page of the book)

PLATE 4

Harlequin Hare

HERE I come, here I come!
     I'm Harlequin Hare!
     I jingle and jangle, tinkle and strum!
I'm mad, and enjoy it! I make them all stare
Turning head-over-heels now and then in mid-air!

     I'm ready and willing
     To box for a shilling,
Can sprint like a flash, and play crazy new tricks;
     If I get in a fix
     What do I care?
     I'm Harlequin Hare!

The madder the gladder's my motto, as all
     Who see me agree;
I prance and I dance, and I caracole on
With cymbals and bells and accordion.
     You can bet that I'll be
In good time tonight for the Butterfly Ball –
     Harlequin Hare
Will be there, will be there!

PLATE 5

Esmeralda, Seraphina and Camilla

ESMERALDA, Seraphina and Camilla
Each a glad and glorious Caterpillar,
A live mosaic of orange, green and gold,
What silks they wear! What gorgeous bags they hold!
But oh, they're slow! – yet safe if they're unseen
By any hungry crow, or other airborne wretch.

Creeping through grasses and the purple vetch
Almost as soundless as the bindweed twining
Among the flowers, with smiling sunlight shining
Through their enchanting parasols, with happy sighs
All three are whispering of that dream-come-true
When they'll be different beauties – Butterflies!

Belles of the Ball they hope to be ("Oh, do
Please introduce me to that lovely Caterpillar").
All Caterpillars have the hugest appetite,
So Esmeralda, Seraphina and Camilla
Can hardly wait to join the Feast tonight

PLATE 6

MAJOR Nathaniel Gnat
With his fine-feathered Cavalier hat
  Is off on a spree,
  So with you or with me
He cannot stop now for a chat.

He sleeps in a four-poster bed
With a canopy over his head,
  He lives in great state,
  He dines off gold plate,
And oh, what a life he has led!

On camels' and elephants' backs
In deserts and forests and shacks,
  In Tibet or Peru
  He has known what to do
In ambushes, raids and attacks.

The call to adventure he hears
Has made him shoot tigers and bears,
  And it quickens his pace
  When a beautiful face
Or an elegant figure appears.

Though asked to the Ball, I suppose
He may visit some lady he knows,
  Look deep in her eyes
  And bewitch her with lies
And present her, of course, with that rose.

PLATE 7

Happy-Go-Lucky Grasshopper

APPY-Go-Lucky Grasshopper
Snatched up a gamp and clapped on a wig,
He doesn't care how he looks,
Just doesn't care a fig!

For hours he's been hopping
Without ever stopping,
Delivering cards for the Ball,
Invitations to each and to all,
And he's taken great care
To plan and prepare
Good things for the Feast, so that every guest
May have for a treat the food he likes best –
Nuts for Squirrels and Worms for Moles,
And little titbits for Beetles and Voles.

Happy-Go-Lucky Grasshopper,
What awful risks he takes!
As Grasshoppers have no brakes
He doesn't always land
Exactly where he planned,
To be happy and hoppy and free
Is every Grasshopper's wish –
Happy-Go-Lucky, STOP! or you'll be
A snack for a big-mouth Fish!

SAFE! He straightens his wig
And breathes a sigh of relief;
The shock was almost too big
For the boatman on his leaf,
But Grasshopper's not afraid in the least
And with hugest hops goes off to the Feast.

PLATE 8

WHEN it's dusk or dark on earth,
Dusky, misty, ghostly,
It's then Magician Moth goes flitting mostly,
Softer than a breath.

Marked with a skull since birth
He knows no fear of death,
And when he folds his patterned velvet wings
Keeps very still, as midnight darkens,
Keeps very still, and hearkens
To the faintest, strangest, and most secret things.

They say that whispers from some very far,
Never-seen and nameless star
Give him power to foresee
Happenings unknown to you and me.

Before the Ball was even thought of, he
Knew just when it would be,
So here he is, in the clear light of day,
Famous Magician Moth outside this place of call,
The busy old White Lion,
Buying a jug of honey, something to rely on
Before he flits away
(But not till after sunset) to the Ball.

PLATE 9

Lizzy Bee

FLOWERS hold for honeybees
 Drops of purest nectar,
 And Lizzy Bee, of all the bees,
Is the busiest collector.

Humming to herself for hours
Lizzy visits many flowers,
Honeysuckle, thyme, and clover;
Yellow pollen powders over
Lizzy's legs, as round she goes
Probing into every rose –
Lizzy knows, Lizzy knows
Where the sweetest nectar lies.

Oh today a big surprise!
Not a single flower will see
Anything of Lizzy Bee;
Today's her happy holiday
(She deserves one day at least),
She's left the hive to buzz away
With loads of honey for the Feast.

PLATE 10

Good Night, Children

I WAS saying Good Night to my children,
 Not old enough to have wings
They're still living under the water,
 The greediest, ugliest things;

"In the lake as smooth as a mirror
 I can hardly believe what I see,
While saying Good Night to my children
 I've fallen in love with ME!"

To the Feast and the Ball have now flitted
 Dragonflies red, green and blue,
You can't spend all night at your mirror
 So what are you going to do?

"Me? As I'm a glittering Beauty,
 Though I too was ugly when small,
Of course I must rush off to show off
 My beautiful self at the Ball!"

PLATE 11

The Rodents' Express

FROM their sharp front teeth to the tips of their tails
The Rodents were thrilled by their trip on the rails
In a Midland express with the *Princess of Wales*.

Rat with his hoop,
Shrew with his nose,
Won't leave the fence
Till they see how it goes.

Mad about trains!
Someone must call
And tell them it's time
To start for the Ball.

Going first-class in the Rodents' Express
Mrs Squirrel had managed to put on her dress,
Her butterfly dress – it's a perfect success!

But Rat with his hoop
Shrew with his nose
Can't be bothered
About their clothes.

"No good scolding them,"
Squirrel explains,
"The plain fact is
They're mad about trains."

PLATE 12

ALL IN red and yellow
Dressed as Punchinello,
Fox, the crafty fellow,
Travelling to the dance
Casts a wicked glance
Through the carriage door
At the prima donna
On the platform there,
Madame Bella Swanna,
Setting out upon a
European tour.
    You may be in danger
    From a handsome stranger –
    Madame, do beware!
As for Lily Lizard,
Silly Lily Lizard,
Did she know the hazard
Going on her own,
Travelling by train?
"Never be alone
With a man unknown,"
So they'd often told her,
"Specially if handsome:
He might be insane,
Might hold you to ransom."
    Fox, he means to hold her.
    When he wants his lunch
    THEN will come the crunch!

PLATE 13

Toad in Bed

"IT'S NO good trying to rush things, is it?"
Said Doctor Vole, making his second visit.
"Tests of your water clearly showed
You'd swallowed some pollution, Toad.
What you now need, as I've already said,
Is to keep snug a day or two in bed.
It's no good fidgeting or cursing.
You're lucky to have splendid nursing
From Cyril Crayfish, your unselfish friend,
And Willy Water-Measurer. You'll soon mend.

"I'm glad they keep your room so nice and damp,
That's very healthy, good against the cramp.
To get you on the way to convalescence
There's nothing like this Anti-Effluent Essence.
There's lots of this pollution now about,
But soon you'll be all right again, and hopping-fit, and out."

PLATE 14

Y NAME'S Aranea (Miss Spider to you),
I'm lucky to know, and I'm lovely to view.
As you see, I am rich. The silk which I spin
Is exceedingly strong and incredibly thin.

My maid, Alice Weevil, so faithful and civil,
Has cleverly brought, as I guessed,
My green-and-gold shoes. I *must* look my best,
Very soon now the Ball and the Feast will begin,
And I mustn't be late.

I still have to make up my eyes
(Unlike you I've got eight).
Alice, what is the time? How it flies!

So do I! Through the air, on a gossamer thread,
I shall glide to the Ball. As I float overhead
All will look up, and the dancers will pause
To give me a deafening round of applause.

Alice, good night. Don't lock the front door
Or sit up for me. I'll be back about four.

PLATE 15

Froggy

DREAMY in the afternoon
Froggy went a-wooing, far
Where the clear-cut hilltops are,
Idly touching his guitar,
Noticed Badger drifting by,
Badger in his striped balloon
To the Ball go drifting by,
Not too low and not too high,
Through the dreamy afternoon.

Where the clear-cut hilltops are
Reflected in the glassy lake
Froggy plucked at his guitar
Through the dreamy afternoon,
Ditties drifting on the wind
Fingers picking out the tune,
Never making a mistake.
(Fox was fishing with a friend,
And they listened by the lake.)

Froggy had set out a-wooing
But having sung and having played
And found that there was nothing doing
Comfortably down he laid
Both himself and his guitar,
Where the spotted agarics are.
On that pillow dreaming, he
Saw uprising, circling, see,
Persons known to you and me.

PLATE 16

The Hornet and the Wasp

INVITATIONS were sent to the Hornet and Wasp
On condition they laid by their stings.
"They might as well ask us," protested the Wasp,
"To fly to the Ball without wings."

"I hate you," the Hornet replied, "but for once
What you say does seem perfectly true.
I'll never go stingless so long as I live
And it *I* get a chance I'll sting *you*."

"This Ball," said the Wasp, "means nothing to me,
And nothing *you* say means a thing,
So long as I'm airborne, so long as I'm armed,
I shall fight for my freedom to sting."

Those who stick to their principles stick to their stings
And those who have guns will take aim,
But after they've stung, or after they've shot,
What they never will take is the blame.

Plate 17

THERE on the bridge
In the middle of the day
Are several of the guests
Who've come a long way,
The sun's overhead,
The shadows are shorter,
And someone says, "Look!
Who's that by the water?"

"That's Mr Kingfisher,
He's a splendid sight
But looks as if he's waiting
And waiting for a bite,
Unlike us he wasn't
Invited to the Ball."
So just to cheer him up
They give him a loud call.

Mr Blue Kingfisher,
Brightest, bluest bird,
Hears what they're saying
But answers not a word,
And waiting for a bite
He may be there all night.

Let him wait and wish!
If you take a look
You can find a fish
That he'll never hook.
Take a careful look!

PS.   *The fish he won't catch you can easily see*
       Outlined up above in the boughs of the tree.

PLATE 18

Sir Maximus Mouse

THAT huge new block, in EC4,
Of the Cheddar Bank they built last June
Has a secret flat, on the fourteenth floor,
For Sir Maximus Mouse, the Cheese Tycoon.

There he sits in his cosy room
With a ticker-tape, in view of St Paul's,
To watch how the market rises and falls.
His whiskers twitch at the hint of a boom,
His whiskers droop at the hint of a slump in his
Hundred-and-twenty super-companies.
As a cat will watch a mouse, he stares
At the ups and downs of stocks and shares,
A prince among mice and millionaires.

"Knock, knock," says the grandfather clock,
"Money's not all, money's not all –
He has quite forgotten the Butterfly Ball!"

Plate 19

The Long-Eared Bat

With the setting of the sun
The Ball has now begun
And those who've not arrived must take care,
Must all look out for *that*
Swift and fearsome Bat
Swooping in the twilight – oh, beware!

After sleeping all day long
Upside down, he's feeling strong
But he's hungry, and he's looking for a bite;
As he wasn't asked at all
To either Feast or Ball

He must snap up little insects while in flight;
Because they rightly fear him
They try not to go near him,
And that smartly dressed Cockchafer
Would be a great deal safer
If he'd taken quite a different way tonight.

Plate 20

Sir Bedivere and the Stag-Beetle

**F**ROM the castle that towers above the trees
Two he-Ladybirds guarding their flock
Heard a hullaballoo. "Jacky, listen, please,
We don't want our sheep to die of shock,
That noise would give even lions a fright."

Someone was roaring, "Raise the portcullis!
Lower the drawbridge! Here comes the Knight!"
Then out rode Sir Bedivere, whirring along
On his Stag-Beetle steed, and singing a song:

"I'm ready to fight
With Red Ants or White,
With Goblins or Elves;
Myself and my Stag-Beetle,
All by ourselves,
We ride off in quest
Of treasures or dangers,
Monsters or strangers,
A fire-breathing Dragon,
A Damsel distressed –
Adventure, adventure, that's what we need,
Myself and my faithful Stag-Beetle steed!"

PLATE 21

Cheers, My Dears

WHEN Newts assemble for a drink
They lap up beer and stout and port
And spirits by the quart,
They'd drink the Atlantic dry, I think,
At least if it were free from salt
And brewed with hops and malt.

With time to spare before the dance
The Newts all gathered took the chance
By a bright fire – well, what d'you think? –
To take a little drink:
They thought that it would give them all
A starter for the Ball.

"Now cheers, my dears," said Mr Newt,
Dressed in his hat and birthday suit,
"We Newts are a good-natured clan,
Much thirstier than man,
So let's see who can drink the most,
To him we'll drink a toast."

They laughed, they sang, the fire was hot,
They lurched, and Father took a fall.
Said Mrs Newt, "Do you know what
You've been and gone and done?
Missed as a Newt, you silly sot,
Our evening at the Ball!"

PLATE 22

The Butterflies' Air-Lift
and the Weevils v. Caterpillars Cricket Match

H OW COULD those creatures that slither and crawl
Ever have got to the Butterfly Ball?
All had been asked and wanted to go
But Snails are so sluggish and Slugs are so slow,
How *could* they have got to the Ball?

"We'll put on an air-lift, I think it our duty,
And ferry them there," said the Camberwell Beauty.
"We'll fly through the sky in this festival weather,
A seven-in-hand all harnessed together,
And *we* can bring *them* to the Ball."

So Swallowtail, Orange-Tip, Peacock and Brimstone,
Purple Emperor, little Chalk Blue,
Brighter than flags of the quarrelling nations
Happily fluttered and peacefully flew,
And ferried the Snails to the Ball.

Did they ever look upward, the watchers below?
Not they, nor the fielders, nor those at the wicket;
All were watching to see how this over would go,
And the Weevils' ace batsman, a demon at cricket,
Was keeping his eye on the ball,
His weevilish eye on the ball.

PLATE 23

The Most Wonderful Tune in the World

THE MOST wonderful tune in the world
(All other claims are false)
Is Simon Centipede's masterpiece,
The Lepidoptera Waltz.

On the night of the Butterfly Ball
We heard the music begin,
Cymbals and harp and drum,
Bassoon, clarinet, violin.

How splendidly Simon plays!
Nothing could be so neat
As the way he strikes the notes
With a dozen or more of his feet.

When the guests began to dance
Even those who had no wings
Flew around, as if in a dream,
On feet like enchanted things.

The dancers went off their heads,
You've never heard such applause
As Simon bowed and bowed
To the storm of "Bravos!" and "Encores!"

When he kissed the Butterfly's hand
And said, "Madam, I wrote it for you!"
Two tears of joy in her eyes
Twinkled like morning dew.

PLATE 24

The Grasshopper's Feast

EVERYONE had heard the Feast would be
Spread out under the broad oak tree,
At toadstool tables here are we
Happily eating, as you can see.

The Grasshopper's given us each a treat
By getting us *just* what we like to eat;
On every table there's different food,
Some to be nibbled, some to be chewed.

Moths and Butterflies suck what is sweet,
Squirrels crack nuts, they don't like meat,
Green stuff pleases Hares and Rabbits,
But some of us Insects have cannibal habits.

Caterpillars keep chumbling away
At nice green salads night and day,
But Moles and Frogs like Worms for their tea –
To eat bread-and-butter they'd *never* agree.

What a lot of trouble Grasshoppers take!
There goes one with a strawberry cake,
And Grasshopper, look, this glass is mine,
Please fill it up again with blackberry wine.

PLATE 25

Shelly Snail and Swallowtail

SWALLOWTAIL:

"SHELLY SNAIL, that mask you hold
Gives you a look that's young and bold;
What are you really like, I ask,
Behind that brightly painted mask?"

SHELLY SNAIL:

"Swallowtail, the real Me
Behind the painted mask you see
(Truthfully I must reply)
Is someone most extremely shy.
I know this is the one great chance
For me to ask you for a dance
And make your harebell girdle swing
While we perform a Highland Fling,
But oh, you lovely Butterfly,
The fact is, I am much too shy."

SWALLOWTAIL:

"Shelly, I understand you well,
You're only happy, I can tell,
When sitting snug inside your shell.
I shan't forget you while we hop
And flutter in the dance, non-stop,
So when you sit and drink your tea
Inside your shell please think of me."

PLATE 26

The Butterfly Ball

THE BALL is beginning! From every direction
Guests are all crowding to join in the fun;
Was ever there seen such a varied collection
Of beautiful creatures? The Ball has begun!
First the Damsel-Flies' Ballet, so nimble on tiptoe,
With glittering wings, and so famous, these four,
They can kick in a can-can, or dance a calypso,
And whatever they do always gets an encore.

When Rabbit and Fox put on different faces
You can't be quite certain whichever they are,
But soon all the guests will be showing their paces
To the loud hurdy-gurdy and Froggy's guitar,
They'll see Aranea on gossamer prancing
Over Harlequin Hare with his one-hare-band,
And Happy-Go-Lucky Grasshopper dancing
With lovely-winged Butterflies, hand in hand.

With Slugs, Mice, Squirrels, and all sorts of creatures,
Ants, Moths and Earwigs the place will be packed,
Some will say, "*Whose* are those faces and features?"
And all will be happy as act follows act.
Each one will feel that this great Ball is bringing
The joy of a lifetime, and all are agreed
With Froggy, who twangs his guitar, sweetly singing
His favourite song that says *Love's all you need.*

PLATE 27

Homeward

SUCH a Ball and such a Feast
 No one can forget:
 Oh, if both would last, at least,
One more hour, not finish yet!

Some are sleepy, some could madly
 Dance away till dawn,
Lovely wings are folding sadly,
One small Ant was seen to yawn.

Now the great big Moon is sinking
 And goodbyes are said,
Darkness spreads, and some are thinking,
"Who will light us home to bed?"

Switching on his greenish light,
 Glow-worm's heard to say
(He's so helpful and polite),
"Let me put you on your way.

"With my light I'll guide you all,
 Homeward, like a friend,
While you're sleeping, Feast and Ball
 In your dreams will never end."

PLATE 28

NATURE NOTES

GADFLY (*Plate 1*)

Gadflies are blood-sucking two-winged flies of the genus *Tabanus*, notably *Tabanus bovinus*, so called because its bites were supposed to make cattle "gad about" the fields with their tails erect. In fact this behaviour is now thought to be due to the attacks of a different but equally pestilential species of fly, the warble fly *Haematopota*. Gadflies belong to a family whose members have acquired many folk names in Britain: horse flies, stouts, burrel flies, dun flies, breeze flies, whame flies and, perhaps most popular nowadays, clegs. Few people can have gone for a country walk on a hot summer's day without having had to repel attacks by clegs on some exposed part of their person.

It is the female gadfly which is the villainess. Males are sedate and rather shy creatures, and much prefer a meal of nectar from a wild flower to sucking blood. They spend their time resting on tree trunks, leaves or flowers, or drinking from a pond or stream, while the females home in on to the nearest warm-blooded animal. It is often a case of the biter bit, however, for gadflies themselves are preyed on by robber flies, dung flies, dragonflies and wasps.

Tabanid larvae appear to need moist conditions to live in, and eggs are often laid on vegetation overhanging water, into which the tiny larvae fall. They are voracious creatures, capable of disposing of two or three worms, two or three times their own length, within a week.

DORMOUSE (*Plate 2*)

The dormouse is the only British rodent that hibernates; and is indeed the only fully hibernating British mammal, for bats and hedgehogs are liable to wake up on warm winter days and feed a little. The dormouse owes its name to this habit, deriving it from the French *dormir* (to sleep); it also has a folk name, "the sleeper". Hibernating animals are naturally adapted to living through the winter, avoiding a period when food is scarce, by becoming torpid and greatly slowing down their metabolism, the temperature of normally warm-blooded animals falling to that of their surroundings. Each autumn dormice fatten themselves up for the winter, and when they waken in spring may weigh little more than half what they did before hibernating.

Dormice live to a great extent in the branches of low trees and shrubs, eating leaves, nuts and various other kinds of fruit. They are also great nest builders', each individual having a summer sleeping nest in the branches and a winter hibernating nest on the ground. Birds' nestboxes may also be appropriated. The breeding nest is often quite near the ground.

The dormouse is a native British animal, but in parts of the Chilterns another species can be found. This is the continental fat dormouse, introduced at Tring, Hertfordshire, at the turn of the century. It makes itself unpopular by entering houses and careering about in roofs, making a noise that has been likened to that of having a herd of small elephants overhead.

MOLE (*Plate 3*)

The mole, an insectivore and allied to the hedgehog and the shrews, is the only British mammal that spends almost its whole life underground. Its bodily structure and habits of life are admirably adapted to the excavation of its network of tunnels, some up to a foot beneath the surface, and to hunting its earthworm prey in them: the flexible elongated snout for probing after food, the strong muscular hand-like forefeet for excavation, the cylindrical body for smooth transit. The soft velvety fur, which bends backwards or forwards as the mole moves up and down the tunnel, is also well adapted to its subterranean life.

Moles are proverbially blind, but in fact are not so, although their eyesight is poor. Three other widely held but equally erroneous beliefs about the mole are that it eats its own weight in food every 24 hours, that it digs incessantly for food, and that if deprived of it for as little as four hours it will die. In fact moles eat only about half their body weight in worms each day, get much of their food by picking it up after it has fallen into their tunnels, have three separate eating periods in the day, and can survive for 48 hours without food. Though seemingly far from agile, a mole has been seen to catch and kill an animal as active as a frog.

Farmers, gardeners and especially greenkeepers dislike moles because of the molehills they throw up in the course of constructing their underground tunnel system. Some molehills are much bigger, and contain the mole's nest, but we still know next to nothing about why some moles make these "fortresses", and others apparently do not.

OTTER (*Plate 4*)

The otter is our only primarily fish-eating carnivore, and as such is regarded with suspicion by anglers and fly-fishermen. However, it is probable that otters eat mainly sick or otherwise inefficient fish, and so on the whole do good rather than harm to fish stocks. They are almost the shyest of our larger native mammals, and few people, apart from anglers, have ever seen one in the wild. Nowadays they are increasingly scarce in the southern and eastern half of Britain, and indeed virtually extinct in many districts. In the north and west, however, otters are still quite frequent. Little is known of the reasons why otters have become scarce, but contamination of our rivers by the residues from farm pesticides, among other noxious wastes, is suspected. At all events, otter hunting has been brought to a halt over a large part of England, for the simple reason that there are no otters left to hunt. Otters breed in holes in river banks, known as holts, and appear to do so all the year round. Within the last ten years they have encountered competition for the fish in our streams from the North American mink, which has escaped from fur farms and established itself widely in Britain. It is smaller and darker than the otter, and has a narrower muzzle and a shorter, less stout tail.

RAT (*Plates 4, 12*)

As with squirrels there are two kinds of rat in Britain, the black rat and the brown rat, both of which are aliens. The black rat, which confusingly can sometimes be brown, but always has a more pointed snout and longer thinner tail, arrived in the Middle Ages, perhaps in the baggage of the returning Crusaders. The brown rat did not reach us until about 280 years ago, and has since driven out the black rat, the so-called "Old English" rat, except in large towns and seaports. The water rat is not truly a rat at all, but a vole. The brown rat is probably the most destructive vertebrate pest in Britain, and it is regrettable that no really humane way of controlling it has yet been found. In the countryside rats would be fewer if game preservers did not destroy their natural enemies, stoats and weasels.

STOAT AND WEASEL (*Plate 4*)

Stoats and weasels are very similar to look at, long, thin, short-legged animals, most often seen as they dart across the road in front of an oncoming car. Stoats are the larger of the two, and have a black tip to the tail. In winter, in the northern parts of Europe, including northern Britain, stoats lose their reddish-brown colour and turn white, although the tail tip remains black, and this winter fur is known as ermine. Weasels are smaller, with no black tip to the tail, and do not turn white in winter. Females, at about 6 inches long, are significantly smaller than males, which measure 8 inches (stoats are 17–18 inches). In some country districts male weasels are called whitricks and females canes, and indeed the early naturalists believed that these were two different species. Just to add to the confusion, in Ireland there are only stoats, but the Irish call them weasels. Stoats feed on animals as large as rabbits, and are well known for their habit of hypnotizing their prey by their sinuous, dancing movements, which allow them to get near enough to pounce. Weasels naturally kill mainly smaller animals and birds, but can deal with young rabbits and are quite capable of attacking rats twice their size. Stoats and weasels should be handled with great care, not only because they can readily twist round to administer a sharp bite, but also because, being relatives of the skunk and the polecat, they can leave an unpleasant smell on the clothes of the handler.

HARE (*Plate 5*)

Hares are perhaps best known for being mad in March, a saying that derives from their aggressive courtship behaviour in early spring. Pairs leap freely about the fields, chasing and "boxing" each other. Two kinds of hare live in the British Isles, the brown hare, widespread in the lowlands, and the blue, or varying, hare, which is more local in the hills of the north and in Ireland. The blue hare gets its second name from the fact that, like the stoat or ermine and the ptarmigan, it turns white in winter, which helps to conceal it against snowy backgrounds. Both our hares are larger than the rabbit and differ from it also in living always above ground; like the rabbit they are herbivores. The place where a hare crouches in the grass during the daytime is known as its form. Although mainly open-country animals, brown hares are also not infrequently seen in woods. The jack hare is the male, females are does and young ones leverets.

BUTTERFLY (*Plates 6, 23, 26*)

Butterflies are a group of day-flying moths – a few other British moths also fly by day. They differ from true moths in having club-tips to their antennae, and no mechanism for hooking their forewings and hindwings together. There are only 68 British species, of which 10 are rare, compared with well over 2000 moths. The Camberwell Beauty is a rare immigrant from Scandinavia, which usually comes over as a pupa with lumber and flies off here when it hatches. It was first seen in Britain at Camberwell in South London in the 18th century. The gaily coloured Swallowtail is a special rarity of the Norfolk Broads. The Peacock has caterpillars that feed on stinging nettles, and the butterflies are often found hibernating in dark corners in houses in autumn and winter. The Brimstone is another hibernator, and like the Peacock is one of the first butterflies to emerge in early spring, usually about the third week in March. Its caterpillars feed on buckthorn. The name comes from its colour – brimstone is sulphur. The Purple Emperor is a rarity, found only in a few large oakwoods in the Midlands and south of England. Its caterpillars feed on sallow, but the butterflies have a depraved taste for descending from their basking places in the tops of the highest oaks to feed on carrion. The Orange-tip is one of our most attractive early spring butterflies. It reveals its relationship to the mundane cabbage whites by the fact that its caterpillars eat the leaves of lady's smock and other plants of the cabbage family. There are eleven species of blue butterfly in Britain, but only the males are blue, though in the Brown Argus the male is brown like the females of all of them. The rare Large Blue has a singular life history. Its caterpillar spends most of its life in an anthill, feeding on the ant larvae and supplying the ants with a honey-like substance from a special gland.

GNAT (*Plate 7*)

Gnats are a family, *Culicidae*, of two-winged flies, the larger members of which are usually called mosquitoes, although the commonest British mosquito, *Culex pipiens*, is confusingly called the common gnat. Gnats are best known for their biting proclivities on warm summer evenings, when the victims do not much care whether they are being bitten by mosquitoes or gnats, but just reach for the insecticide spray. Winter gnats, however, do not bite people. These are the gnats which can be seen dancing up and down in small groups as if suspended on strings like tiny puppets, right through the year. They are more conspicuous in winter because there are so few other insects about. Fungus gnats also dance in swarms; their larvae feed on fungi and decaying vegetable matter. One of the most curious gnats is the so-called phantom midge, which has a completely transparent larva, also known as the ghost or glass larva.

GRASSHOPPER (*Plate 8*)

There are about a dozen different species of grasshopper in the British Isles, all mainly herbivores. They are related to the tropical locusts, and are distinguished by their overdeveloped hind legs, which enable them to jump considerable distances. Male grasshoppers make a stridulating "song" by rubbing their hind legs against their forewings. Stridulation is also a characteristic of the closely related crickets, which can be distinguished from grasshoppers by their long antennae, among other things. The great green grasshopper, at well over an inch long the largest British grasshopper, is actually a bush cricket. Its ears are curiously placed just in front of the knee joint of its front legs.

DEATH'S-HEAD HAWK-MOTH (*Plate 9*)

This is the largest British moth, having a stouter body and broader wings than the perhaps even rarer Convolvulus Hawkmoth, whose wing-span of 4–5 inches is about the same. It was given its macabre name by the English entomologist Moses Harris in 1778, because of the supposed likeness to a skull-and-crossbones of the markings on its thorax. For this reason, and because it can make a shrill squeak by forcing air from its air sacs through its proboscis, the more old-fashioned country people still regard it with grave suspicion. The caterpillar, which like most hawk-moth caterpillars has a horn at the rear end, is perhaps more often seen than the moth itself. It feeds on potato leaves, and in a good year quite a number turn up when the potatoes are being harvested.

HONEYBEE (*Plate 10*)

Honeybees are among the most social of all insects, with an elaborate hierarchy of queens, the dominant fertile females, drones, the subordinate males, and workers, the numerous infertile females. There are no genuinely wild honeybees in Britain today, but as honeybees are not truly domesticated, but merely use hives provided by man, they roam freely about the natural environment in search of honey and pollen for food. Worker bees usually attack and sting humans only in defence of their hives, and queens rarely do even this. They reserve their venom for other queens, but if a virgin queen enters an occupied hive, she will usually be attacked and killed by the workers before she can endanger the reigning queen.

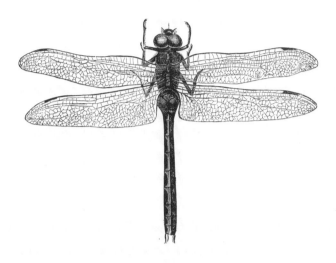

DRAGONFLY (*Plate 11*)

Dragonflies have a fearful reputation in country districts, where they have such names as "horse stingers" and "devil's darning needles". They are, however, quite harmless to human beings, and for that matter to horses, being unable to bite or sting. This is no consolation for their small insect prey such as midges and mayflies, however, for they are ferocious predators, especially the large kinds known as hawkers and the smaller darters. Even the delicate small dragonflies known as damsel-flies have habits hardly appropriate to damsels. Most dragonflies spend most of their time close to fresh water, although the emperor and some of the large hawkers, being strong fliers, may not infrequently be seen well away from it. In the larval stage, dragonflies are completely aquatic, their larvae, known as nymphs or naiads, being equally ferocious predators on smaller water creatures. There are about 5000 species of dragonflies in the world (only a tiny proportion of the million or so insects of all kinds), of which 43 occur in the British Isles. Dragonflies are among the most primitive of insects, having existed for well over 200 million years. At this early date, when the coal seams were being laid down in northern France, giant dragonflies occurred with a wing-span of 27 inches, making them the largest insects ever known to have existed on earth.

SHREW (*Plate 12*)

Shrews are not rodents, like rats and mice, but insectivores, related to the hedgehog and the mole. They have much the same tapering snout and soft dark-grey velvety fur as the mole. As the name insectivore suggests, they are eaters of insects and other invertebrates, and voracious eaters at that. They are restlessly active little animals, and because of their extremely high rate of metabolism quickly die of starvation if they cannot find a constant supply of food. Even so they rarely live for much more than a year. It used to be thought that shrews died of shock on being handled, but it is now known that they actually die of starvation through not being fed enough in captivity. There are three British species: the common shrew, the one most often found lying dead; the pigmy shrew, the smallest British mammal; and the much larger water shrew, the least common of the three.

SQUIRREL (*Plate 12*)

Squirrels are rodents, but of a different family from rats and mice. There are two kinds in British woodlands, the native red squirrel, easily told by the hairy tufts on its ears, and the North American grey squirrel, which has been established here for at least one hundred years, and may in summer appear distinctly rufous. The grey squirrel is in fact one of the classic instances of the danger of introducing alien animals into strange environments. It has now become a serious pest, endangering the re-establishment of broad-leaved woodlands over a large part of England. The red squirrel, once common over the whole of Britain, is now found mainly in Scotland, having been replaced over most of England and Wales by the American invader. Squirrels do not truly hibernate (see under Dormouse), but are less active in very cold weather, wisely retiring to their dreys (nests) until it gets warmer.

Fox (*Plate 13*)

The fox is our only surviving wild member of the Dog Family – once we had the wolf as well. Although popularly supposed to subsist on a diet of the farmer's chickens, foxes are actually omnivorous, eating almost anything from bilberries to young rabbits, and from dor-beetles to carrion. Undoubtedly they also take a few sickly or new-born lambs, more in some districts than others, but the good shepherd and the careful henwife can usually avoid serious losses. Foxes are most attractive animals in their own right, and there is a small but growing army of fox watchers, who lie up near their earths and watch the fox cubs come out to play on warm – and sometimes cold – spring and early summer evenings. Foxes have two characteristic calls, the high-pitched and often triple bark of the dog fox, as the male is known, and the loud wail or scream of his mate, the vixen. This scream can be an alarming experience if heard close to, sounding uncannily like a human being in dire distress.

SAND LIZARD (*Plate 13*)

The sand lizard is the rarest of our three native species of lizard, the two others being the common lizard and the slow-worm, which looks like a snake but is actually a legless lizard. The sand lizard is only found on heaths in the south of England and on sand dunes on the Lancashire coast. It hibernates during the winter months, and after mating in May and June, eggs are laid in June and July and the young emerge in August. Sand lizards eat all kinds of small invertebrates, but mainly insects and spiders. When eating the larger grasshoppers and beetles they remove the hard wing-cases first.

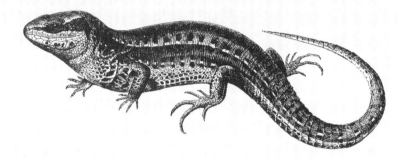

CRAYFISH (*Plate 14, with medicine*)

The crayfish is the largest freshwater crustacean found in the British Isles, somewhat resembling a miniature lobster. It is not to be confused with the crawfish, which is in fact a species of lobster and is purely marine. The crayfish favours especially rivers and streams on chalk and limestone soils. Crayfish are regarded as delicacies, and are still occasionally eaten in Britain. At one time there was a regular fishery for them on the Thames. Crayfish were caught, among other methods, by working an osier twig into a noose, and gently looping it over the creature's claws. Today numbers are gradually decreasing, probably largely due to pollution and habitat destruction by "improvement" of rivers. Crayfish are also a favourite food of the otter.

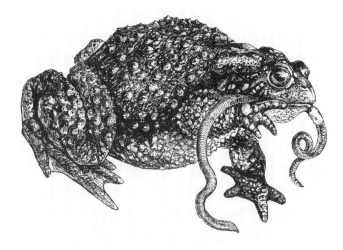

TOAD (*Plate 14*)

Toads owe the worst of their reputation to the fact that they secrete a poison in the warty glands that are scattered over their bodies. They are voracious creatures, eating, according to one 19th-century naturalist, "all living animals that are susceptible of being swallowed". They appear to have an almost unlimited appetite. The large toads of southern Europe will even eat mice. There is a second and smaller species of toad in Britain, the attractive little natterjack, found mainly in coastal areas of north-west and eastern England, and inland on the sandy heaths of the Surrey/Hampshire border. Toads, like frogs, pass through a tadpole stage, but their eggs are laid in strings, not amorphous masses.

VOLE (*Plate 14*)

Of the three species of vole that inhabit the mainland of Britain, much the commonest and most widespread is the field vole. The two others are the bank vole and the water vole or water rat. Voles are easily told from mice by their blunter muzzles. Field voles sometimes swarm in plague proportions, and then attract large numbers of the birds of prey that regularly feed on them, especially short-eared owls, hen-harriers, and kestrels. They are vegetarians, and during a plague may do great damage, not only to grassland but also to young plantations, where they kill or deform the young trees by nibbling off the bark. The water vole is much larger than the other two; there is a not infrequent variety that is completely black.

WATER-MEASURER (*Plate 14*)

Bugs to some people mean all insects, to others just one species, the bed-bug. To entomologists, bugs are all the members of the order *Heteroptera*, to which the bed-bug belongs. One of the more specialized members of this order is the water-measurer or water-gnat *Hydrometra stagnorum*, with long legs that enable it to stalk about the edges of ponds and ditches in search of the smaller creatures that form its prey. It is not to be confused with two other kinds of water-bug, the water-skaters *Gerris*, with equally long legs, which glide over the surface of still water, and the water-boatmen *Notonecta*, which propel themselves underwater with their powerful hind legs.

MONEY SPIDER (*Plate 15*)

Money spiders are a large family of about 250 species of tiny spiders, *Liniphiidae*, comprising some two-fifths of all the spiders of Britain. They exist in very large numbers. It has been estimated, for instance, that over a million money spiders of various kinds inhabited a single acre of a grass field in Sussex in the autumn. These are the spiders whose webs are so conspicuous on dewy autumn mornings, slung between grass stems and on other vegetation and glistening in the early morning sunshine. These webs are sheets or hammocks of silken gossamer. The spiders themselves at this time take off and drift for considerable distances on their gossamer threads.

FROG (*Plate 16*)

Frogs, like toads and newts, are amphibians, formerly also called batrachians, a class of cold-blooded vertebrates that differ from the reptiles both in having a softer skin and in needing to resort to water to breed. Amphibians also differ from reptiles in passing through a gill-breathing tadpole stage between the egg and the adult animal. A frog's eggs are embedded in a gelatinous cover which is 99.7 per cent composed of water. They are laid in a large sponge-like mass, known as frogspawn. The tadpoles at first consist of little but a head-and-body and a tail. As they gradually develop into frogs, they acquire legs and lungs and lose their tails and the gills that enable them to breathe under water. Frogs hibernate under water, either in the mud at the bottom of ponds or in holes in the bank beneath the surface. Male frogs croak in the spring, usually in chorus, and both sexes grunt. There is only one native British frog, but two species have been introduced and are established locally, the edible frog and the marsh frog, the latter being especially common on Romney Marsh in Kent. Both these are much louder croakers than the common frog.

HORNET (*Plate 17*)

The hornet is a very large wasp, indeed the largest species of British wasp. It has a fearsome reputation, as the phrase "stirring up a hornets' nest" indicates, but in fact does not attack man unless provoked. Of course, if you do poke at a hornets' nest, you are asking for it. These nests, like those of the common and German wasps, are usually made of chewed wood-pulp, inside a hollow tree, but occasionally in a house roof. Female hornets are about an inch long, with the body coloured dull orange and brown, instead of the sharply contrasted black and yellow bands of the two wasps. Hornets are no longer among the common insects of the British countryside.

WASP (*Plate 17*)

Entomologists recognize enormous numbers of wasps as members of the order *Hymenoptera*, to which bees and ants also belong. But to everybody else, "the" wasp is what entomologists regard as a group of six (in Britain) insects with bright black and yellow bands on their bodies. These are the creatures that raid the family jam-jar and may cause trouble at teatime in the garden in late summer. The two commonest are the common wasp *Vespa vulgaris* and the German wasp *Vespa germanica*. Their bright colours are another instance of warning coloration. Actually, despite their superficial nuisance value, these wasps are useful to man, feeding largely on flies and other less desirable insects. They are highly social insects, living in communities like, but less complex than, the honeybee, and make large rounded nests of wood-pulp, which they chew into a grey papery substance, and which are to be found either in a hole in the ground or hanging up in a tree.

KINGFISHER (*Plate 18*)

The kingfisher is one of the most brilliantly coloured birds in Britain, and belongs to a widespread family found mainly in the tropics. It fishes by perching on a branch overhanging the water and plunging in when it sees a minnow or other small fish. It also takes crayfish and other larger aquatic invertebrates. Sometimes the kingfisher will hover instead, and dive down like a miniature gannet. When it catches a fish, it beats it on a branch or rock to stun it and stop it wriggling, and then swallows it head first. Kingfishers nest in tunnels in the banks of rivers, and their nests are notoriously evil-smelling after a young brood has been raised on a fish diet.

MOUSE (*Plate 19*)

Mice are rodents, like rats, and so are primarily vegetarians, though they will also eat a good deal of animal food when they come across it. There are four British species, the all-too-common house mouse, which is found out in the fields far more often than most people realize, and is of course a regular inhabitant of corn stacks – if such things still exist in a mechanized agriculture. The commonest mouse of all is the wood mouse or long-tailed field mouse *Apodemus sylvaticus*, which forms the staple diet of many birds of prey. Much rarer is its relative the yellow-necked mouse, *Apodemus flavicollis*, distinguished by a broad yellowish chest band. The tiny harvest mouse is our smallest rodent, though not our smallest mammal (see pigmy shrew). It is increasingly rare to find its remarkable little ball of a nest slung among the corn stalks.

COCKCHAFER (*Plate 20*)

The cockchafer or maybug is a large bumbling beetle that makes a humming sound on spring evenings. Both the adult and the larva are exceedingly destructive insects. A swarm of adult cockchafers can strip the leaves off a tree in one day. Each female lays about seventy eggs. The resulting larvae, known to farmers as white grubs or rookworms (because rooks like to eat them), live for nearly four years underground feeding on the roots of crops, herbaceous plants, trees and shrubs. Rooks may take a certain amount of grain, but this is more than made up for by the good they do in keeping down wireworms (the larvae of the daddy-long-legs or crane fly) and cockchafer grubs.

LONG-EARED BAT (*Plate 20*)

After the tiny pipistrelle, the distinctive long-eared bat, with ears an inch and a half long, is the commonest British bat. Quite recently it has been discovered that there is a second species of long-eared bat in Britain. This is the grey long-eared bat, *Plecotus austriacus*. It has darker fur on its face, but its identification is really a matter for museum experts. Bats are the only true flying mammals, in so far as they use flapping and not just gliding flight. They feed very largely on winged insects such as moths and beetles caught in flight. The cries of bats are so high-pitched that most older people can no longer hear them. Each squeak lasts for 1/500 of a second, and when bats are excited they may utter 200 squeaks a minute. The echoes of these squeaks are used by bats in a form of natural sonar to echo-locate their prey. Despite the old saying "blind as a bat", bats have perfectly good eyesight.

ANT (*Plate 21*)

Ants are highly organized social insects of the family *Formicidae* in the order *Hymenoptera*, to which bees and wasps also belong. The thirty British species mostly live in underground nests, but some, such as the yellow hill ant *Acanthomyops flavus*, make the anthills found in many grassy places. The large wood ant *Formica rufa* also builds large heaps of wood fragments and dried leaves up to 4 feet high. Ants are divided into fertile males and females, which are winged, and infertile females, which are unwinged and called workers. There is a mass emergence of winged ants in late summer, when the fertile pairs first mate and then tear off their own wings. The so-called "ants' eggs" fed to fish are not eggs but cocoons, in which the grubs or larvae are transformed into adults. Ants have many strange habits. Some farm and milk aphides for their honeydew. Others capture cocoons from smaller ants' nests and use the resultant workers as "slaves". The thief ant *Solenopsis fugax*, the smallest British ant, lives in other ants' nests and steals their food.

LADYBIRD (*Plate 21*)

Ladybirds are small beetles of the family *Coccinellidae*, usually red or yellow in colour and spotted black. There are 45 British species, whose Latin names often reflect the number of black spots they carry on their wing-cases. Thus the common two-spot ladybird is *Adalia bipunctata*, the ten-spot ladybird is *Adalia decempunctata* and another species with 24 spots rejoices in the fantastic name of *Subcoccinella vigintiquatuorpunctata*. The best-known fact about ladybirds is that their larvae eat plant bugs, especially aphides and scale insects, and so should be encouraged in the garden – the use of DDT sprays, of course, being a notable discouragement. A ladybird lives for about three weeks as a larva, when it may eat several hundred aphides. This is followed by a pupal state of about one week, the whole cycle, from egg-laying to adult hatching, taking from four to seven weeks.

Ladybirds have a curious habit of assembling together in large numbers, often on a post or fence. This is probably because they are unpleasant to the taste, as indicated by their bright warning coloration, and a large splash of the warning colour warns predators off more effectively.

STAG-BEETLE (*Plate 21*)

There are two species of stag-beetle in Britain, the large *Lucanus cervus* and the smaller and oddly named *Dorcus parallelipipedus*. The large one is the stag-beetle, its male having mandibles quite remarkably like the antlers of a stag (though a stag with rather a poor head, it might be thought). Female stag-beetles and both sexes of the lesser stag-beetle have much less complicated mandibles. Incidentally, stag-beetles do not attack people, but of course a finger put between their mandibles may get nipped. The larvae are white and crescent-shaped, with rufous heads, and spend their lives masticating wood inside rotten trees.

London is the metropolis not only of man but also of the stag beetle, which is commoner in its southern suburbs than anywhere else in Britain. The 16th-century German artist Dürer, with his meticulous draughtsmanship, drew a fine likeness of a stag-beetle.

NEWT (*Plate 22*)

Newts are amphibians, like frogs and toads, which means that they pass through a tadpole stage, when they breathe underwater through gills. They lay their eggs singly on the leaves of aquatic plants, often wrapped up in a little "package". After the breeding season they wander away to find some safe place on dry land to hibernate for the winter. It is not uncommon for them to take refuge in the cellars of houses at this time. There are three kinds of newt in Britain: the widespread common newt; the great crested newt, which is equally widespread but less frequent, and is the largest European newt; and the palmate newt, much the rarest of the three, which is the smallest European newt.

In spring the males of all three species develop a conspicuous crest along the back, and parts of their bodies turn reddish or orange.

CENTIPEDE (*Plate 24*)

Centipedes are among the forty-odd species occurring in Britain of the *myriapods*, a class of invertebrates of equal status to the insects, both groups being members of the arthropods. They live under stones, logs, dead leaves and similar debris, and feed mainly on smaller invertebrates. Different species of centipede have varying numbers of legs, but the British species have between 15 and 101 pairs. Probably the most familiar centipede in Britain is the warm brown, rather flattish *Lithobius forficatus* – it has no vernacular name – which is often seen in gardens. It ranges from 18 to 30 millimetres in length, and has 15 pairs of legs.

MUSK BEETLE (*Plate 24, playing violin*)

The musk beetle is a handsome green longhorn beetle, with red spots on the elytra (wing-cases), and antennae which in the male are one and a half times as long as the body. It may, however, vary in colour from coppery red to bright blue. Its name derives from the strong musky smell emitted by both sexes. The larvae live in the wood of old rotten willows, and consequently the beetles are usually found near willow trees. The musk beetle is one of the most widespread British beetles, and is usually to be seen in July and August.

THE GUEST'S EATING HABITS (*Plate 25*)

Animals must of necessity eat either animal or vegetable food, because minerals provide little or no actual nutriment. All animals appear basically to need proteins, carbohydrates, mineral salts, vitamins and water. There is a distinction between the vegetarians (top right-hand table), such as the rabbit, hare, vole, mouse, rat and squirrel, all rodents in the broad sense, and the flesh-eaters (top left-hand table), such as mole, hedgehog, shrew, frog, stoat and weasel. But many flesh-eaters, such as fox and badger, are in fact omnivorous, taking animal or vegetable food indiscriminately, as they find it. Insects, of course, have quite different methods of eating from the vertebrates, and are in turn divisible into vegetarians, flesh-eaters and omnivores. Most insects (centre table) have mouth-parts designed to bite or chew, but do not have teeth like mammals. Some insects, however, use a siphoning apparatus, and others have developed techniques of lapping up their food. A distinctive insect method of feeding is the use of a piercing device to reach the food supply, coupled with a means of sucking it up, comparable to the use of a straw to drink liquids (bottom table).

SNAIL (*Plate 26*)

Snails, together with slugs, are gasteropod molluscs, mostly of the order *Pulmonata*, breathing through lungs not gills. They secrete a mucus, which they lay on the ground before them to form a track on which they walk with their single creeping foot. This mucus hardens, so that the snail leaves a trail behind it. The most familiar species of snail is the common garden snail *Helix aspersa*, which was formerly eaten in parts of Britain, as it still is on the Continent. One of the few advantages of living in a district where atmospheric pollution is bad is that you do not have these snails in your garden, eating your choicest plants. The snail really beloved of gourmands, however, is the Roman snail, the largest British species, so called because it is often found near Roman remains, and is believed by some to have been originally introduced by them for culinary purposes. However, these snails have been found in pre-Roman deposits, and, so must have been here before the Romans. Nowadays Roman snails are mainly found in chalk and limestone districts, especially the North Downs of Kent and Surrey, and the Cotswolds.

FIREFLY (*Plate 28*)

Fireflies are not flies but beetles, and foreign beetles at that. However, there is one British member of the firefly family which we call the glow-worm, though it is not a worm. The misnomer is excusable because the female glow-worm, which is luminous, is rather worm-like, or at least grub-like. The light, with which she attracts the unlit but more beetle-like male, is produced by the oxidization of a compound called luciferin and its reflection by means of minute urate crystals. Glow-worms are thus luminous (not phosphorescent, which means light produced by previously absorbed radiations). They usually inhabit grassy and heathy places, but are much less common nowadays than they used to be, perhaps because of the large amount of insecticide residues now found in the environment.

ALAN ALDRIDGE AND 'THE BUTTERFLY BALL'

Oliver Craske

HE children's masterpiece *The Butterfly Ball and the Grasshopper's Feast* was created by Alan Aldridge between late 1971 and 1973 in the calm of rural Norfolk.

"I ended up buying a ridiculously large house and realising I could try to be a new Beatrix Potter," he recalls. "It was a new type of thinking for me – that I didn't need to be looning around town, working twenty hours a day. I realised that most of the work I'd done up to that time was done overnight."

Alan had been the rising young star of London's commercial graphics scene in the 1960s. Despite no formal art training, he achieved rapid success with his designs and illustrations for magazines, book covers, adverts, record sleeves and posters. In the opinion of George Perry (who collaborated with Alan on *The Penguin Book of Comics*), "The Sixties, as far as graphic design in Britain is concerned, divide into the pre- and post-Aldridge eras."

In 1966, at the age of 23, Alan was appointed art director of the fiction list at Penguin Books. His radical approach produced some brilliant covers, although some authors found his designs too racy. After two years at Penguin he left to set up his own design studio, Ink. Thereafter he became closely identified with the music industry, his surreal, psychedelic airbrush style a natural with many famous bands of the time. He was a creative consultant to The Beatles' company Apple, and edited two best-selling volumes of *The Beatles Illustrated Lyrics* – the work which he was best known for, before *The Butterfly Ball*. During this time he also worked for The Who, The Rolling Stones and Cream, and produced a notorious poster for Andy Warhol's film *Chelsea Girls*.

After The Beatles had split up and Apple contracted, Alan turned his attention to children's books. He found initial inspiration in Sir John Tenniel's illustrations of

Lewis Carroll's works. Reading that Tenniel had declared himself unable to depict "a wasp in a wig", Alan took up the artistic challenge. He was soon to discover the 1807 classic by William Roscoe, *The Butterfly's Ball and the Grasshopper's Feast*, considered the first British children's book to eschew moral instruction. In a recent survey of the treasures of the British Library, Philip Howard has written, "This book arrived as a revolutionary relief from hellfire and moralising. It is fun and fantasy… the Adam and Eve of anthropomorphic animal fantasy for children."

"I'd go to the British Library's round reading room about twice a week," says Alan, "and order any book on Victorian illustration I could get hold of. So here was this book by Roscoe. It didn't work for me as a poem, but it worked as an idea for a summer's day: these creatures having a ball. I made it that all the creatures were going to celebrate a day of peace, to lay down their stings and fangs – I thought I'd get a bit of an angle to it."

Alan spent the next year preparing the twenty-eight illustrations. First he planned the story and structure of the book and decided on the main character for each page, the additional characters and details of the settings. After that he prepared highly-finished line drawings and then passed them to the airbrush artist Harry Willock, his key collaborator. Each pencil drawing that Alan supplied to Harry was marked with a colour code instructing him in the required colours and where to blush them together. Once the airbrush colours were in place, Alan would sometimes work with gouache to finalise the pictures. The results shone with a sumptuousness reminiscent of the golden era of illustration led by Edmund Dulac and Arthur Rackham.

The appeal of *The Butterfly Ball* illustrations is partly rooted in the sense of mystery and darkness that coexists alongside sheer fantastic exuberance. They are mad, magical and surreal, qualities that children have long embraced in their reading, and that appeal to many adults too.

"I would never condescend to children," Alan said in a 1985 interview. "I just tried to bring out the best of my abilities within the confines of what I'd chosen to illustrate. The passion and the madness I brought to the pictures came through honesty."

Armed with some early plates, Alan approached Tom Maschler, legendary publisher at Jonathan Cape. In his memoir, Maschler recalled the book fondly, describing it as "the cornerstone of a new graphic revolution", but Alan remembers having to work hard to overcome the publisher's caution.

"Tom Maschler told me, 'Look, Alan, the pictures are wonderful but there's no money in children's books. I don't think this is going to work.' So I told Tom, 'I'll get a promotion going. All you have to do is print it.'"

With the publisher confirmed, the book now needed a poet to write the new verses. Alan's first choice was W. H. Auden, but he declined. His second choice was John Betjeman, recently installed as Poet Laureate.

"The pair of us would meet regularly, every Tuesday and Thursday in town," says Alan, "and we'd talk about Highgate, Victorian plumbing or Victorian architecture – but we never talked about *The Butterfly Ball*. We'd go off at twelve, have a few ports, mutton or beef at his local pub, he'd fall asleep by three o'clock and I'd go home – and it would go on forever."

With the deadline looming, it became apparent that Betjeman would not take part. Maschler's solution was to recommend William Plomer, a poet and novelist who also happened to be a reader for Cape. Old school in style, and seventy years of age, Plomer could hardly have been more different from Aldridge, but he delivered on time, penning delightful poems to match the illustrations. The book also featured notes by the wildlife expert Richard Fitter on every animal depicted in the illustrations, a continuing source of pride for Alan.

As the September 1973 publication date approached, *The Sunday Times*, for which Alan had produced many illustrations in the Sixties, honoured the book with the front cover of its magazine, a twelve page article inside and an offer allowing readers to buy six signed prints.

"The prints just flew out," says Alan. "It was phenomenal. We ended up printing 25,000 copies of the book in the first edition – sold out in three days. Over the year we did 600,000 or 700,000 copies."

Sadly, at the moment of triumph, a tragedy struck: William Plomer died on the day of the book launch, on the eve of becoming a best-selling author.

The Butterfly Ball won the 1973 Whitbread Children's Book of the Year award. There were two sequels, *The Peacock Party* and *The Lion's Cavalcade*, and many spin-offs. Roger Glover, who had recently left the band Deep Purple, made an album of rock music based on the book for a planned animated feature. The music was well received, but in the event only an animated short was made, accompanied by Glover's song 'Love Is All'. Glover also organised an all-star performance of the album at the Albert Hall in 1975, which was later released as a film. An audio recording of the book was issued too, featuring Judi Dench and Michael Hordern. There was also *The Butterfly Ball* merchandise, including toys, paint-boxes, mugs, note-pads, calendars and posters.

After drawing the cover for Elton John's 1975 album *Captain Fantastic and the Brown Dirt Cowboy*, Alan had the idea for an animated *Captain Fantastic* feature film, a kind of *Yellow Submarine* for the Seventies. Courtesy of Universal Studios, he spent two years developing the idea before it was dropped. In the meantime, he edited a book of illustrated lyrics by Elton John's collaborator Bernie Taupin, and produced another children's book, *The Ship's Cat*, written by *Watership Down* author Richard Adams, followed by *Phantasia*, a kind of autobiography in verse and illustration.

Since then his career has diverged from book illustration: "Amazingly enough I became known as a script technician. I would do a lot of storyboarding, treatments. CBS got hold of me to develop a book called *Faeries* by Brian Froud, and we made a half-hour show for television. The head of the company liked my thinking and gave me an open cheque to come up with some other ideas – all kinds of wild stuff – and he bought all of them. I settled down in Hollywood, and I've been busy ever since."

That Alan Aldridge has forged a successful career in a distinct field should not be surprising (he has also published a fantasy novel, *The Gnole*), for throughout his career he has, through determination and adaptability, made the most of his talents. But it is as an illustrator that we know him best. John Betjeman said of Alan that "no one comes close to matching his influence on illustration in the twentieth century". *The Butterfly Ball* stands as his most widely cherished creation.

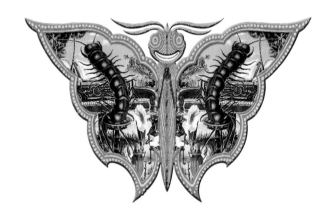

ANSWER to Dandy Rat and the Footpads puzzle:
In the trunks of the trees, if you stand on your head,
His name (which is Max) can clearly be read.